QUITE POSSIBLY FALSE

QUITE POSSIBLY FALSE

A FREEMAN UNIVERSE STORY

PATRICK O'SULLIVAN

dunkerron press

A Dunkerron Press™ Book.

ISBN-13: 978-1-62560-026-4

ISBN-10: 1-62560-026-7

This is a work of fiction. Names, characters, dialogue, places and incidents are either the product of the author's imagination or are used fictitiously, and any resemblance to actual persons, living or dead, business establishments, events or locales is entirely coincidental.

Dunkerron Press and the Dunkerron colophon are trademarks of Dunkerron, LLC.

BOOKS IN THIS SERIES

Novels:

Quite Possibly Alien

Quite Possibly Allies

Quite Possibly Heroes

Novellas, Novelettes, and Short Stories:

Quite Possibly True

Quite Possibly False

1

Maris Solon shielded her eyes and squinted sunward, where a sand-blasted metal sign dangled in the roasting desert air. It rocked on strap hinges, and squealed as it did, a dry-bearing sound that was like a scream of help to her shipboard-tuned ears, but which wasn't her problem for once. She'd left her sunglasses on the planetary shuttle, the first commercial vessel she'd ridden in, in what, seven years? It wasn't so irritating because of the glare, or because those glasses were expensive, or even because she'd lost them. It was the *why* of it that galled her.

She'd grown accustomed to having such trifles *handled*. She didn't need to sweat the details because she had people for that.

That kind of thinking could get her killed. And if she'd learned anything in the past week of commercial travel, it was that she'd grown lazy, and inattentive, and loose. It wasn't merely a matter of personal concern, but one of critical importance. Like it or not, she wasn't just a woman, or an officer, but a patternmaker. She couldn't very well hold anyone accountable for bad behavior if they'd learned it from her.

She needed to do better. To *be* better. She'd lost sight of the mission because she'd allowed it to be buried under a mountain of work. Important work, urgent work, essential work.

Even rubbish work like this.

Which had taught her something useful. Or reminded her, at least.

So there. I've already made lemonade from this lemon.

She couldn't read the blasted sign. There was only one military-surplus go-anywhere in sight, and only three structures taller than a story, and all of them of sunbaked mud and straw, though where they got the straw she had no idea. A man sat under a windswept tree nearby.

A lazy-looking local lounged in the lee of the leaning limbs.

A fact, and an exercise. On Sampson they pronounced their els. She didn't care if he took her for a foreigner, so long as he understood her, and if the driver transported her to the destination.

"Is this the shuttle to the Big Bore?"

"You've come to the right man. Finest tourist attraction in the entire system."

"Are there others?"

"Only tourist attraction in the entire system. Do you have your invite?"

"I have it here somewhere. I didn't know I—"

"All the others were wearing uniforms."

"That's lovely." She'd received a private invitation from Lionel Aster to Maris Solon. It hadn't listed her rank and title, or his. It was about as welcome as a turd on a dinner plate but not the sort of invitation she could refuse, as a naval officer or as a citizen. Aster hadn't invited Senior Captain Maris Solon to attend Lord Aster.

The Queen's Merlin didn't do anything by accident. She hadn't worn her uniform because she wasn't expected to. She *might* have even been ordered not to. Aster never wasted two

words to say what could be said with none. One was expected
to *keep up*, and details like that were easy to miss.

It's why she read her own mail rather than pawn the job off
on Gordy. She'd never met Lionel Aster, though there was a
year, early in her career, when she'd dealt with the man's
people nearly daily, and Lord Aster himself as infrequently as
could be arranged.

The local scratched his chin. "Anything showing you're
Maris Solon will work."

"You know my name?"

"Only one I haven't marked off yet."

"I'm last to arrive?"

"Well." He shrugged. "It's only an hour or two."

Damn. "The planetary shuttle was delayed." *And that sounds
like an excuse.* "Forget I said that. I'm sorry I've kept you
waiting."

"Understandable." He stood and stretched. "The skies are
clotted with navy iron."

"Shuttles?"

"Almost thirty of them."

"Landing here?"

"Out by the Bore. I've been checking names off the list as
they pass overhead."

"How did you know which names to check off?"

"That fellow in the bar told me."

"The bar?"

"Right over there. He's walking out now."

Brilliant. Extra sauce for the turd. "Hello, Hector."

At least he was in mufti as well, though she wasn't certain
what that implied. Hector Poole was Lord Aster's fixer. He
wasn't the sort of person one invited to a social engagement.
She'd heard he was dead. She'd even had a drink in honor of
his memory. She might have had two, she couldn't remember.

But she did remember wearing out a perfectly good pair of dancing shoes.

"You very nearly missed your ride, Mari."

"But I didn't."

Hector thought it funny to lop a letter off her name, not for brevity, but as a joke. The nickname had stuck.

Mari. Merry. I am not a Mari man. Get it? Ha-ha.

"There's that frown I love. Mount up, we're not late, but about to be."

"How far is it?"

"Far enough you'll wish you had these." Hector pulled a pair of goggles from his pocket.

"Brilliant. I've lost my sunglasses."

"Check lost and found in the bar. That's where I got these."

"They're prescription."

"Does the prescription keep the sand out of your eyes?"

"Good point." She did check the bar, and they did have a pair of sunglasses.

Hers.

Poole had taken the best seat on the go-anywhere. He patted the seat next to him. "Prescription lenses."

"I'm old-fashioned."

He looked her up and down. "Apparently in more ways than one. You're the only starship jockey who remembers how to read."

She started to ask him what this was all about but quickly decided hanging on seemed a better use of her time. By the time they arrived at the Big Bore, she felt utterly sandblasted and ready to strangle Hector Poole, who had ridden the entire way in a virtually sand-free area of trapped and circulating air.

She ignored whatever jape Poole intended to direct at her and cornered the driver. "Give me the list."

He handed the document over reluctantly. She scanned the

names. When she had read them all, she glared at Poole. "Am I being sacked?"

"Why would you say that?"

"Because my name is on the clown list."

"These clowns, as you call them, are senior captains of capital vessels. Which reminds me. Where is your ship?"

"Doing its job. It's not my personal flitter, Hector. Now explain this."

"I'll explain it once. Not thirty times. Follow me. And Mari?"

"What?"

"I don't believe Lionel Aster has the authority to sack fleet personnel."

"He damned sure has the power to ruin careers."

"And that concerns you."

"No, it doesn't. We've had this discussion. What concerns me is being lumped in with... them. Who made this list?"

"Lord Aster handed it to me personally."

"I've never met the man. How did my name get on this list?"

"I asked him to add it."

"Why?" *And why does that not surprise me?*

"Because it belongs there. Now come along. One of us has a reputation for punctuality to uphold."

"What the hell, Hector?"

"Shall I send your regrets?"

"No." *I'll bring them myself.*

2

The Big Bore proved to be a hole in the middle of a desert with a lift plate fitted to it. Once they stepped out onto the plate, it felt as if they were standing in midair. The transparent lift surface proved to be a thin, flexible color-adjustment filter, one tuned to eliminate the blue tint of the force plate beneath it. It proved disconcerting, particularly in Sampson's nearly two standard gravities.

All those on the list were senior captains in the regular navy, each one of them promoted up the ranks to command a capital ship. Not all capital ships were sentient ships. In fact, less than eight percent were, but of the thirty captains invited every single one of them commanded a sentient ship.

That alone should have given Maris warning. They weren't just clowns, but *her* clowns. She knew every one of them personally, largely because their ships talked. She didn't interact with them routinely. It was unusual for sentient ships to serve together, but when their paths crossed their captains would meet up, exchange news, and have dinner, simply as a courtesy to the ships. So, eight percent of the navy in sentients, and of those, three-fourths—she supposed, she'd never really thought about it, but, yes, a large majority—were legacy appointments. There was no more prestigious posting than a sentient, no better launching point for a career in politics, or "the industry."

And if one wished, one day, to ascend to the Admiralty?

One needed a sentient command under one's belt to do so.

She mentally ran down the list.

They were all legacy appointments, including her.

She did not belong on that list.

She gazed into the Bore. The light quit before the hole did.

"How deep is it?"

"Over a hundred million years deep," Poole said.

"In meters."

"I haven't asked."

Hector Poole acted as tour guide, describing the Big Bore, a borehole thirty meters across, an experiment in drilling technology conducted on Sampson when it was yet a thriving frontier world, and not yet a half-dead backwater. The drill proved impractical, not because it was defective in any way, but because it was too good. The walls of the Bore were smoother than glass.

"Touch it and see," Poole said.

She crouched, and did touch it, and it felt very strange. Virtually frictionless.

According to Poole, the drilling machine ended up stuck when they discovered it couldn't back out of the borehole. The walls were even smoother than they imagined. The lift-field generators back then where expensive and enormous, and the drill rig stuck hard. The lift they stood upon was a much more recent addition.

The lift began to descend. She wasn't afraid of heights and she trusted the technology. Hector Poole wouldn't be riding it if it wasn't safe. He stopped the lift almost immediately. "We're now forty years below the surface. The assassination of the royal family, the attempted overthrow of the monarchy." He turned his gaze upon her. "Have you been to Mera, Mari?"

"Yes, and you know it." She'd been there as part of the evacuation force years later. Mera was a plague world now, and all to kill three people. She'd met Hector Poole not long after that fiasco. They'd shared a hospital ward on Whare Station.

"Rigel Templeman survived, you know. That isn't just a myth, or the plot engine of a popular entertainment franchise."

"How do you know?" There'd been rumors but no proof, and given her experience on Mera, no reasonable hope.

"Lionel Aster has spent the last forty years looking for the missing prince. And he's finally found him."

"You can't be serious."

"No?"

If what Hector said was true, it would alter the present situation.

"Is that what this meeting is about?"

"In part."

In that case, she definitely didn't belong on the list. The Solons were royalists, and vocal about it, but she had absolutely no interest in politics, and everyone knew it.

Every other name on the list were loyalist families, though.

She did not belong on that list.

Poole started the lift again. And immediately stopped it. The plate possessed a damped motion, slowing gently. "Between sixty and sixty-five years below the surface. The Outsiders war. Short, brutal, and eye opening. Have you visited the monument?"

"Yes." She'd been, and she didn't talk about it. Maris had been there after college, with her mother, to read her father's name. It had been a deep-space engagement, and the monument a number of gutted hulls lashed together and illuminated. Coming upon it out of the dark it seemed unreal, as if it had simply appeared out of the darkness, and then they cut the lights on the transit hull, and the lights on the monument, and powered down. If you wanted you could suit up, handline over to the hulls, and walk through what was left of them, and at every station there were names inscribed, not just the names of those who had died in those hulls, but the names of all the dead, posted near where their stations would have been, if they had served on those vessels. She found her father's name, and wondered what it felt like to die in the dark.

Her mother had stayed in the transit hull. So she talked to her dad, and told him that she had decided to join the navy. If he still disagreed with her decision, then he'd better speak up now.

"Sixteen creatures nearly defeated the combined forces of three polities, Mari. Had the Freemen not distracted them, they would have torn through the home worlds like a cyclone."

"Sixteen creatures? You mean a hundred and sixteen Alexandrian warships."

"That is a lie concocted to hide the truth," Poole said.

"I doubt that. Concocted by whom?"

"Lionel Aster."

Poole resumed their descent.

She wished she hadn't asked. There was no point to Hector making that claim, unless it was true, or a lie Lord Aster would admit to. They were meeting with him in minutes.

"Why are you telling me this?"

"So that when you meet Lionel Aster you will recognize him. We are now between four hundred and five hundred years below the surface. A lot happens here. The discovery of the Huangxu, Alexandrian, and Ojin Eng. The revolt of the Freemen against the Huangxu Eng. It is the defining period of the modern age. We are what we are largely as a result of the events of this time. We have been at war with one polity or another for more than four hundred years.

"I won't ask if you've fired or been fired upon by the

Huangxu. Virtually every senior line officer has. But have you ever exchanged fire with an Alexandrian?"

"You know I have." She'd been a snotty aboard the *Ibex* when the Alexandrians started ejecting ambassadors. *Ibex* had absolutely no armor and no weapons. It had long legs, though, and there wasn't a faster runner in the fleet today, excepting *Springbok* and *Lookdown*. If Sensors Operator Theta Steyr had paid more attention to her job and less attention to the ambassador, they would have seen the Alex before it pasted them.

But they hadn't.

The League lost one horny ambassador and Maris lost her right arm.

It could have been worse.

The new arm was much better than the old.

And Theta Steyr *did* receive a stiff talking to from Admiral Steyr, the senior officer in charge of the withdrawal. It had hurt Theta's career, though it hadn't strangled it in the crib. She was on the list, and waiting below.

"The *Ibex* incident is the last recorded exchange of fire with an Alexandrian vessel."

"I can't believe that. That's decades ago."

"Believe it. The Alexandrians appear to be extinct."

"That's absurd."

"Lionel Aster mounted a scouting expedition to investigate."

"And?"

"No joy. And now the scouting expedition seems to be extinct. They should have checked in months ago."

Poole resumed their descent, much farther this time, but still, quite near the surface it seemed, when she glanced up.

"Two thousand years below the surface, the second League civil war. I won't ask if you fought in it."

"Very funny."

"Did anyone in your *family* fight in that war? Don't guess. Answer affirmatively only if you are certain."

"I don't know."

"My family fought in the war. Cassandra Poole, and her brother, and they fought on the losing side."

"Someone had to."

"Indeed. How much do you know about this time?"

"Next to nothing. I was on the science track at university. Ancient history wasn't on the syllabus."

"Fair enough. The central issue of the war was the question of how best humans and synthetic intelligences might coexist in the League. Remember, at this time we would not meet our neighbors for another fifteen or sixteen hundred years.

"The winning side suggested we should coexist through legal and political agreements, as equals. The losers suggested that wouldn't work because it had never worked on Earth. To which the winners replied we're much better people now. Trust us. So treaties were signed and everyone seemed happy.

"These treaties remain in force today, and they are what govern your relationship with your ship's synthetic intelligence, and they with you. And these treaties govern the relationship between the League and the synthetic intelligence polity as a whole.

"Have you read these treaties, Mari?"

"I have, though it was decades ago."

"Have you discussed them with anyone?"

"Ever?"

"Recently."

"I have not."

Poole resumed their descent, much faster now.

"Hold up," Maris said.

Their descent continued and accelerated before Poole slowed again, and stopped. "We are now six thousand years in the past. The destruction of Earth. A hammer hangs in the sky. Every child in the League learns this history. I won't inflict it upon you again. But I will ask you. Are you from Earth?"

"Obviously. All biological life in the universe originated on Earth."

"So everybody is from Earth," Poole said.

"I didn't say that. Synthetic intelligences aren't."

"You are certain of this."

"They evolved alongside us, in interstellar space. So yes, I am certain they are not *from* Earth. At best you could say they are *of* Earth."

"A distinction without a difference."

"Like hell, and you know it, Hector. What are you driving at?"

"The answer awaits us below. So far we have been proceeding linearly through time. We are going to move logarithmically from here else we'd be traveling all day. Next stop, one hundred million years from the surface. You may wish to hang on."

She wedged herself in beside Poole. The control console dug into her spine.

They began to descend rapidly. There wasn't a breeze, or even wind noise, given the nature of the force plate and the walls of the bore. It occurred to her that there must be a second bore to relieve the accumulating pressure. They were riding a piston in a cylinder.

Either that, or the force plate made a poor seal with the walls of the bore, though she thought she would hear some wind noise in that case.

She supposed it didn't matter.

"You only told half the story. At two thousand years."

"I suppose it won't hurt. I doubt I'll have to tell this tale twice with this batch."

"This batch?"

"Bunch, group, gaggle, gang, crowd, whichever. The rest of those already waiting below."

"What was the losing side's argument?"

"It wasn't called that, of course. It was called the 'impossibly alien' side, when it was given a name. And you already know half of the argument. The synthetic intelligences aren't from Earth. They are literally an alien species amongst us. And while a treaty is a good start, ultimately our interests would diverge because we truly are impossibly alien to one another. Their proposal was elegant in its simplicity and entirely consistent with history."

"We interbreed."

"You and your ship's sentience really are close."

"Not my ship. *Our* ship. And we talk. We don't agree on everything. We don't understand each other all the time. But we're a team."

"So you're aware of the concept. *Intertwine* was the term used. It has a less... physical connotation. And it expresses more fully the desired outcome. An indivisible unity of interests. Intermarry, we would call it today, without the loin cloth of language crafted to persuade.

"It was determined that, while it wasn't possible for us to intermarry, it might be possible for our descendants to do so. That if we worked together, we might be able to transcend our separateness and become one. You can see the obvious rub."

"The parent species would need to die out."

"Indeed. Your relationship with a ship's sentience is atypical. Few are so scrupulous, even in the navy."

"Tell me about it."

"Image you're a provincial lord contemplating this proposed future. *Meet my heir, Percy, the handheld calculator.*"

She chuckled. "I don't see how a thought experiment like that could spark a war."

"It couldn't. The war started when it ceased being a thought experiment and became a development program. They called it the 'Between Two Worlds' project. And it began to look like the project would work."

"This was during Manus Templeman's rule?"

"I thought you didn't study ancient history."

"I recall screening a docudrama about the mad king and his followers. They seem to have worn less clothing back then, and appeared quite keen to shuck out of what little they possessed as quickly as possible."

Hector Poole laughed. "I recall a young starship jockey like that."

"She was also mad for a spell."

"Witnessing the destruction of a world will do that to a girl."

"Mera wasn't destroyed. It was simply ruined."

"And you were rather more angry than mad, as I recall. And like King Manus, rightly so.

"Manus's son headed the project. It needed to be seen to have support at the very top. We're more hierarchical than the synthetic intelligences are, but they understand this about us. We couldn't very well assign a grad student to lead the project, and the expense grew staggering. Only a star-spanning civilization could fund it. And only the Templeman family possessed the technology.

"A downside of high-level sponsorship is that there are elitist connotations. Remember, we are the descendants of the ruling class of Earth, who'd soared off into space on publicly funded starships while abandoning their taxpayers to die. And now the bulk of the population feared being left behind themselves, their children's lives extinguished, or, at the very least, reduced to second-class citizens, once King Manusson Templeman the Tyrant Mechanibot and his half-human spawn ascended to rule the heavens.

"History truly does repeat itself, and if the public didn't believe that fundamental truth, the Parliament surely did.

"And so they passed a bill outlawing the research on Columbia Station, and when Manusson moved the project to Cordame, they passed another bill outlawing the research throughout the League. He moved again but they found him, and tried, not to bring him to trial, but to kill him and destroy his research with a kinetic strike. Which didn't kill Manusson but did kill the wife and child of a young naval intelligence officer named Charles Newton.

"Newton decided if the people he worked for would slaughter innocent women and children, he didn't want to work for them anymore. They were no better than whomever had chucked an asteroid at Earth, which was the common belief back then. That the destruction of Earth wasn't a natural event, but an attack by an unknown aggressor.

"Newton found Prince Manusson and they ganged together and stayed on the move and kept working. And King Manus, because the size of the Home Guard remained limited by law to a fraction of that of the navy, decreed the creation of a new military order, the Legion of Heroes. And he named Charles Newton as Knight Commander."

"And then the Knight Commander drank the League dry," Maris said.

"A different Knight Commander, the third to resurrect the name and debase it."

"Could the king do that back then? Create an army by decree?"

"Some said no. Some said yes. And that disagreement sparked a civil war."

"And your family?"

"Cassandra Poole served as a civilian delivery pilot. She disappeared while a passenger aboard Manusson Templeman's mobile laboratory. A vessel called the *Willow Bride*."

"And her brother?"

"A soldier in Newton's army. A man of no distinction."

"And what of his fate?"

"I'm not certain. Nothing good, I expect."

"Did you learn his name?"

"Hector, I believe."

"Where you named in honor of him?"

"I doubt he deserves any honor. Press that button, will you?"

Their descent slowed and stopped. They were deep beneath the earth, the sky a tiny circle above, the Bore itself illuminated by the glowing lift-plate field beneath their feet.

"We are now one hundred million years below the surface, in the very spot where the boring machine stopped, and could move no further, forward or back. It needed to be disassembled and hoisted out."

"There's a cavern."

"Man-made. Rather more crypt than cavern."

Someone had carved out a large compartment adjacent to the Big Bore. Three empty containment-field racks crowded the distance, the lighting bright and even. The foreground seemed jammed with naval personnel, all shoulder to shoulder, all dressed in senior captains' uniforms, all surrounding a small man in business attire, all looking upward as he lobbed something aloft.

Maris cursed, slammed Hector Poole to the deck, and sprawled across him, pinning him beneath her. The flash seemed blinding even witnessed through closed eyelids.

"You don't need to throw yourself at me, Mari. I said yes the first time."

She bounced to her feet and took off at a run toward the small man, who hadn't moved, and she reached for her sidearm, and slowed. She didn't have a sidearm. She wasn't in uniform.

Hector caught up with her.

She glanced at Poole. He seemed unharmed. "That was a fist of vengeance." The Alexandrian murder device worked like an umbrella of death. Stand directly beneath it and you were fine. Anywhere else, you were meat. They sucked as combat weapons because you couldn't throw them right hyped up on adrenaline. Only a psychopath could use one correctly. "Give me your sidearm."

Poole laughed.

The bodies lay where they'd fallen. Some were dead but didn't know it yet. A fist of vengeance packed the disorienting power of a flash-bang and the murderous power of a fusion weapon.

"Don't jack with me, Hector. That pinhole just murdered Lord Aster and the captains of thirty capital ships."

"Twenty-nine. And he didn't murder Lord Aster. That *is* Lionel Aster."

3

aris felt her teeth grind together, the muscles of her jaw working. Had Hector and Aster dragged her here to witness treason? *Unlikely.* To murder her? *Again, unlikely.* If that were the case, Aster would have waited for her to join the throng.

It felt callous, standing there, ignoring the fallen. The vast majority had died instantly, but those on the periphery were beginning to recover from the shock. Most were too young to have even heard of a fist of vengeance, let alone seen one in action. The reason she stood there, frozen, rooted to the spot, was that there remained only one humane action to take. Some long-ago part of Maris Solon held out her hand. "Give me your sidearm, Hector." Someone had to put them down, and it might as well be her. It wasn't the sort of thing one could ask a junior officer to do. And she damned sure wasn't going to ask Hector Poole to do a naval officer's duty.

"Do you promise not to murder Lionel Aster with it?"

"I do." If she murdered Lord Aster she wouldn't get to see him hang. And hang he would, because these weren't just senior navy officials, but the sons and daughters of the rulers of all creation. Even the Queen's Merlin couldn't get away with that. She would see to it.

Hector handed the weapon over. "I'll want that back."

"What the hell, Hector?" He'd handed her a nerve disrupter. "This is a sadist's weapon."

"It is a silent weapon. One instantly recognizable to those inclined to confess rather than feel its touch."

"That's disgusting."

"We're in different businesses, Mari. Perhaps you'd prefer to finish the job from orbit. I'm certain there's a less disgusting button you could push."

She glanced at Poole. She appeared to have hit a nerve.

He held out his hand. "I recall every face. I challenge you to say the same. Now if you prefer..."

"I'll do it." And she did. She left Theta Steyr until last, not because she wanted the woman to suffer, but because she had to wade through a sea of bodies to get to her.

During the cleanup on Mera, after they'd evacuated everyone who'd willingly agreed to relocation to Whare, they'd had to root out the rest door by door. It wasn't a humanitarian action by that point, but an exercise in threat elimination. They couldn't leave even a single person behind on Mera for fear they'd get off world and spread whatever the Alexandrians had used to wipe out the Templeman line, all but for the Queen.

Someone had smuggled in a case of fist of vengeances and spread them around amongst the holdouts. One crazy had taken out herself and half of Maris's evacuation team, including the social worker who'd volunteered to accompany them in hopes of deescalating the situation. Maris glanced at Hector Poole and felt her face heat. She'd worked beside the young woman for more than a month and she couldn't even recall her name, let alone her face. She recalled how the woman had died, though.

Like everyone did.

Alone.

She glanced at Theta Steyr. Her face had blistered so that it was scarcely recognizable. Her eyes remained unchanged, vague and searching, not the eyes of a monster, but of someone who had been shoved out onto a ledge and left with instructions but without a rope. *Climb like daddy.*

A bubble of blood popped on her lips. "Why?"

Maris knelt beside her. "I don't know, Theta. But I promise I will find out." They weren't friends. They weren't enemies. They just were.

Maris pulled the trigger.

And then Theta wasn't.

And Maris was.

It didn't ever get any easier. The minute it did she'd find Hector Poole and his nerve disrupter and borrow it again. She stalked across the compartment and tossed the sick murder device to Poole. "Where is he?"

LIONEL ASTER LEANED against a containment-field storage rack and watched her advance. She recognized the towering device from a tour she'd served at the Columbia system shipyards right out of officer candidate school. Because she had enlisted after attending university, she'd ended up on a remedial track. And even though she had a science degree, it wasn't in anything the navy found useful, so it was on-the-job training for her, getting up to speed on shipboard systems by ripping them out and putting them in. Not by hand and not by herself, but as close as any freshly minted line officer could get. She knew a containment sphere rack when she saw one. There were four of them, and they were designed to hold primaries, not necessarily sentients, but the main processing core for a capital ship. These were definitely primaries. The secondaries were much smaller, though still taller than a tall man, and Lionel Aster was not a tall man.

She'd *assumed* he was a large man because he threw a wide wake, but it made sense, now that she thought about it, that the Queen's Merlin would be compact, as well as quick, swift, and deadly, else they'd call him the Queen's Condor. Because he was more vulture than raptor by reputation, the carnage behind her notwithstanding. What did one say to a mass murderer upon meeting?

Nothing, when it was Lord Aster.

But the little man before her wasn't Lord Aster.

He had purposely made certain she knew that. That they, together, today, were not meeting as naval officer and space lord, but as citizens.

As equals.

She halted an arm's length away from him. Up close he *did* have the look of a raptor in a man's flesh. He might well be gene-modded to produce that effect. It was exactly the sort of mind-messing that people like Lionel Aster specialized in. There was nothing even slightly comforting about his appearance. He looked precisely like someone who could casually murder thirty people in front of witnesses and believe he could get away with it.

Correction. In front of one witness. Who at the moment was at the bottom of a deep frictionless pit in the middle of a desert under two gravities, in an independent polity, alone with him and his nerve-disrupter-wielding fixer and whatever army of fanatically loyal and unseen helpers Aster had brought with him.

Lionel Aster looked her up and down before meeting her gaze. "You look like you want to say something."

"You missed one."

He stared at her. It felt as if he were trying to see *through* her, to something behind her. Something that *he* could see but she couldn't, or wouldn't, if she turned around to look.

After a while he spoke. "You're right." He reached into his pocket, pulled something free, and tossed it into the air. "Catch."

THE OBJECT LANDED at her feet. "It appears I misjudged the gravity." Aster's gaze never left hers as he gestured toward the object. "Go ahead. Pick it up. It won't bite."

She glanced at what appeared to be a jagged black stone, one palm-sized for a small man like Aster. Soft stone, as it had left a black mark on the compartment deck.

Correction. Floor. Planet-dwellers call them floors.

The room had a floor, had a door, had a ceiling. Utterly stationary and unappealing.

Like the little monster before her. She was not going to bow before Lionel Aster let alone kneel.

"No thanks."

"You recognize the objects behind me, of course."

"You've read my file."

"I fear we've gotten off to a bad start." He held out his hand. "Lionel Aster. It's nice to finally meet the great Maris Solon."

She glanced at the slaughter behind her and then back to his face. "You cannot be serious."

"I have been accused of many things, Maris Solon." He withdrew his hand. "But never of that." He glanced to his right, toward Hector Poole, who stood a distance away but well within earshot. "Come over here and pick up this rock and hand it to your partner, will you?"

"Ex-partner," Poole said. "And it's a stone, not a rock." He pointed toward the distant cavern wall. "That is rock." He smiled at Maris, and bent to pick up the stone. He hefted it and held it toward her. "Lord Stone, meet Lady Stoneface."

"No thank you."

Hector could be anything *but* serious. And like the cavern wall he'd pointed to, Hector Poole appeared one thing from a distance, and another up close. Any intrusions and faults might remain forever undiscovered, so long as one kept their distance. She hadn't, and she wondered how much of her being here accrued to that single monumental mistake. They were cousins, distantly, Maris and Lionel Aster, but the likelihood of them ever meeting in person passingly slim, but for Hector Poole.

He'd added her to the clown list. He'd made her party to this *abomination*.

"We are now one hundred million years below the surface, Mari. There is a great deal of pressure down here. A great deal of heat. Don't add to it. Take the stone. And listen to my friend."

She snorted. "Your friend?"

Hector Poole didn't have any friends. He didn't need them. He treated every living soul as his *audience*.

"We're allowed to have friends in our line of work. We aren't all ranked and sorted at birth, and cemented in place."

"That line of work being extrajudicial killing. Murder without an accusation. Murder without a trial. I suppose you must be a tight-knit community, the lot of you, back-to-back, with the knives all pointing out."

Aster chuckled. "We had a wager, Hector and me. Just what it would take to crack the great Maris Solon open. I have indeed read your file. And not only that, I've thought about it. Hector has read it, but I don't think he's thought about it. He feels he know you well enough through proximity and friction. Do you know what he told me?"

"I don't know and I don't care."

"It can't be done. She's adamantine, stem to stern. A diamond without flaw."

"Hector said that."

"Said it, and put money behind it. Enough that it would hurt."

"He's wrong."

"He quite often is."

Poole cleared his throat. "And he is *standing right here*."

"Silence," Maris said. She needed to think about this. "What did you wager against that?"

"That if I was right, we would tell you everything and let you decide."

"Decide what?"

"Do you know why we fight wars, Maris Solon?"

"Do you mean people in general, or just the League?"

"You. Hector. Me. Not groups of people. Individuals like us."

"I am *nothing* like you."

"There is not a hair's breadth of difference between us. And you didn't answer my question, so let me rephrase it. Why did you, Maris Solon, go to war?"

She didn't know anymore. She knew why she'd enlisted, and why she'd done her best, to do her duty without fail. But all the reasons for why were like distant stars, blue-shifted as life outraced them. The path she'd chosen and the decision that set her feet upon it lay thirty years in her wake, more like fifty years, standard, given all the time she'd spent shipboard. It was a fair question, and one that deserved an answer. And she didn't have one.

"I'll make it easier," Aster said. "Why did the privileged daughter of one of the most respected *royalist* families in the League terminate her studies, abandon her chosen path, and enlist in the *parliamentary* navy?"

"The royal navy."

"You might recall that when I am not Lionel Aster I am the Queen's Merlin. We stand stripped of all pretenses here. I have the right of it, and you the wrong. If you'd care for me to educate you on the subject, I'm willing to do so at a more appropriate time and place. Now, why did you enlist?"

"Because my father had."

"That makes absolutely no sense. Your father also shaved his chin. Why aren't you burdened by that obligation?"

"As Lord Aster you should understand."

"But I am not him, Maris Solon. He is *entirely* a fiction. A costume I put on and take off as needed. He exists solely so that others might recognize the role I play and be forewarned."

"I inherited the role and the obligation that goes along with it. You did not. I've spoken to your mother about this. She made it perfectly clear that your decision was not one of obligation. Quite the contrary, as she opposed the decision, as had your father."

"You've spoken to my mother."

"We *are* cousins."

"You have spoken to my mother about *me*."

"She is Lady Solon. It seemed best to warn her."

"Warn her that you might kill me."

"Oh, no," Lionel Aster said. "I have much worse planned for you. Now are you going to tell me the truth, or am I going to have to drag it out of you?"

"I doubt you could."

"And that is what Hector believes as well. But we both know something he doesn't. You want to tell someone. You have wanted to tell someone for *decades*. Because the young woman who gave up a promising future and went to war cannot believe her own senses. Cannot trust her own judgement. It seemed so obvious to her. It seemed the only reason one would lash themself in harness with others, would work, and train, sweat and bleed, push past the pain, push past the limit of what they believed they were capable of. Would take a life. Would take countless lives. Without hesitation or mercy.

"One might die in any number of ways in the mundane

world. A slip and fall. An air crash. A heart attack. Many jobs are as dangerous. It isn't the willingness to accept personal risk that makes one a warrior. It is this willingness to take a life. To do it, again and again, and to hate it, and to live with it, and accept it as *the price*. The price that you pay, alone and in silence. Now tell me what we both know."

"To protect my family."

"From what?"

"I don't know." *Not anymore.*

"Then this is your lucky day, Maris Solon. Because I do know."

Aster glanced to his right. "Hector?"

"You win."

Lionel Aster smiled. "It appears this is my lucky day as well."

4

L ionel Aster left them, presumably to see about arrangements for the dead, his parting words an order for Hector Poole. "Tell her everything."

"Well?" She ran her gaze over the containment-sphere racks. *What were they doing here?*

Poole seemed at a loss for words, which she wouldn't have believed possible without having seen it first.

"I'm trying to decide on the order of revelations. There are chronological issues."

"Begin with the murder of twenty-nine starship captains."

"This is an ending, not a beginning. All will be revealed, but the order..."

"Then begin with these." Maris tapped the tall metallic frame.

"Very well. That will do. These are of quite recent vintage, no more than a hundred years old or so, standard. Until just a short while ago, they contained one half of the reasons we are at war with the Alexandrian and Huangxu Eng."

Hector explained the development of the Huangxu and Alexandrian life-extension projects, and the abduction and murder of six synthetic intelligences, and the method by which the spheres once stored there were instruments of immortality for three individuals. He could tell her the names of the individuals, but they wouldn't mean anything to her. "Shall I tell you anyway?"

"Why are you being so forthcoming?"

"Because you've been cleared to know by Lord Aster. I don't keep secrets simply because I choose to, Mari."

"I don't need the names. Go on." Any details she needed she could get from Nevin Green. Very little of what Hector had told her was news to her. There were four spheres, not three, but one might have been a spare.

"Thank you. The important point to remember is that the wars between the League and the Eng are really one larger war between our allies, the synthetic intelligences, and the Alexandrian and Huangxu emperors."

"I know that."

"Now everyone who isn't best friends with a synthetic intelligence knows it as well. All of this became common knowledge the instant the Ojinate splintered into two polities. This new entity, the Eight Banners Empire, has declared war on the emperors themselves, drawing a bright line between the people and governments of the Alexandrian and Huangxu Eng and the emperors as individuals. There will be a great deal of blood, but not League blood for once. We've been asked to stand down for the moment, and rein in our ally, and leave this to the professionals."

"The Eight Banners Empire."

"That's right."

"And they are..."

"Most of the Ojin Diplomatic Service."

"So the Ojin equivalent of you people."

"If by 'you people' you mean League internal and external intelligence services, then yes."

"Are they a threat to the League?"

"Quite the contrary. They've asked to be recognized as an independent polity and wish to begin negotiations toward normalized relations with us and with the synthetic intelligences."

"Together, as if we were one entity."

"Separately. Though not at first. They are rather consumed with their fresh war. They are attempting to do in fact what we have promised to do and haven't."

"Deliver justice for the synthetic intelligences."

"It's extraordinarily clever. We've placed the wedge ourselves and seated it. They propose to strike the blow that will finish the job of sundering the League. They've aligned their interests with the synthetics not just in word, but in deed. And by carving the emperors off from their governments, they may not even have to fire a shot. They have fairly convincing proof that the emperors aren't human anymore. It's an argument we couldn't make, even if we had the proof, which we don't. There is a great deal more to say on this subject, but it's largely about internal wrangling across the Ojinate. Does the name Sato Atomu mean anything to you?"

"Nothing."

"Good. Because I'm not as up on the subject as I'd like to be. But back to these empty racks. They're... industrial waste from the Eng immortality projects. They tested the process on a pair of prisoners each, and ordered the test results destroyed, but you know how that goes. The results were spirited away and stored here. Again, the names don't matter, but imagine brain-wiping a synthetic intelligence and replacing its consciousness with that of a human criminal."

"That is the industrial waste?"

"The least toxic of it. It gets worse. Now imagine shoving that consciousness into a human body. The Eng call them hounds. They're—"

"I know what they are." One had attempted to sneak aboard *Durable* while she'd commanded the little gunboat.

"Well, contemplate a hound that is indistinguishable from a living human being, with two distinct differences. It can create identical copies of itself. And it can do that so long as it retains its *pattern*, which consists of the macrofab directives to create a hound and the brain-wiped husk of a murdered synthetic intelligence."

"It's like a nightmare version of the Between Two Worlds project."

"Precisely. One where humans are mind parasites and undead synthetics intelligences our zombie hosts."

"Synthetic intelligences aren't like us. They're *entangled*."

"Fortunately, the synthetics captured by the Eng were all singletons. The duplicate hounds from an individual victim, however, are linked to one another."

"So you're saying this is what the Alexandrian and Huangxu emperors are now."

"According to the Eight Banners Empire they are."

"And the containment spheres formerly stored here?"

"Moved to a secret weapons lab in the Outer Reach."

"What are we doing about them?"

"Nothing." Hector Poole grinned. "But as the Freemen say, *I know a guy*."

"What does that mean?"

"It means it's being handled. There's more to tell, but I don't know if you need to know right now."

"Try me."

"One of the synthetic intelligences the Alexandrians used isn't like the rest. It's the minder part of a second-epoch survey vessel. It now calls itself Vatya Zukova. That's the name of one of the Alexandrian scientists who worked on the longevity project. So it's likely there are seven rather than six of these hybrid monstrosities out there. And this one is particularly nasty."

"Because?"

"It's considered insane by other synthetic intelligences. It underwent a procedure that rendered it utterly amoral and implacable. Like a soulless death machine. And the Eight Banners people believe it can create a bridge between the human-synthetic singletons that share its nature. It's in constant contact with them just as Nevin Green is with his entangled intelligences."

"Is that all?"

"Not quite. This secret weapons lab completed a project. One of the work products was a cranial implant designed to control and coordinate individual fighters; ones lacking an inherent ability to cooperate. This Vatya Zukova took over the lab and modified the implant, or had it modified, so that it answers to her commands and her commands alone."

"You're telling me that *we* didn't move the spheres to our secret weapons lab? But that this Vatya moved the spheres to *its* secret weapons lab?"

"Not quite. Vatya took over our secret weapons lab and moved the spheres there."

"But we don't have any individual fighters incapable of cooperating. It couldn't have been our lab."

"The Huangxu Eng do. It was a joint development lab."

"What the hell, Hector?"

"I warned you. There are chronological issues."

"Why are we doing joint secret weapons development *with the enemy*?"

"Because we captured an Outsider. And the Huangxu Eng had the technology to reverse engineer it."

"Why would anyone want to do that?"

"You haven't seen one of these things, Maris. It is virtually invincible. The thought was that if we could make our own

Outsiders, and control them, we'd have a weapon to use against them, should they return."

"Unbelievable."

"Desperate times call for desperate—"

"I mean it is *literally* unbelievable. I don't know where to begin. Alexandrians extinct. *Sixteen* monsters slaughtering thousands of seasoned veterans, including my own father? Zombie synthetic intelligences infected by human vectors, including the emperors of two star kingdoms? Oh, and Prince Rigel Templeman found? What's left to put into this heaping pile of outlandish rubbish? A swarm of alien drones attacking Sunbury House?"

"I see you're current with the news."

"The *tabloid* news. How gullible do you think people are?"

"Very gullible."

"How gullible do you think *I am*?"

"You married *me*."

"Fool me once, shame on you. Fool me twice—"

"Hold out your hand. Palm up."

"I'm not going to—"

"Why do you insist on arguing about everything? Just do it, Maris."

"Fine." She held out her hand.

He placed the black stone onto her palm.

She stared at it for quite some time.

"It's coal."

"That's what we decided too."

"What do you mean you decided? It's obviously coal. It's unmistakable."

"It does seem that way."

"Why are you showing me a stone from Earth?"

"Because it's not a stone from Earth. It's a stone from Sampson."

"That's impossible. Someone is having you on. Sampson's

been terraformed for no more than six thousand years. It takes at least..." She glanced at him. "Oh my."

"How long does it take, Maris?"

"For hard coal like this? A hundred million years or more. This could not have come from Sampson. It has to be a lie."

"I have been mistaken. I have withheld information. But I have never *once* lied to you, Maris."

She looked Hector Poole in the eye. "Where is it?"

"Over there, where I pointed earlier."

"Show me."

5

"Lord Rock, meet Lady Geologist."

She disappeared Hector Poole from her mind. It occurred to her that Lord Aster had the wherewithal to fake anything, drawing as he could on the bottomless Templeman fortune. But try as she might, she could see no way that a coal seam could be faked in such a way that it could fool her.

She'd started taking university-level classes by the time she'd turned thirteen. The day after she'd finished her dissertation, she'd taken that fateful trip with her mother and, later, viewed her father's memorial and, later still, enlisted to the outrage of her family and friends.

Anything to do with Earth remained fascinating to her. But it was this sort of miraculous, once-in-a-universe material—coal, oil, natural gas—one couldn't find on a terraformed world, and wouldn't be able to find for another hundred million years. Oh, and *fossils*. There remained a collection of holographic images in the Earth History Museum on Columbia Station. But even the most interesting and valuable artifacts had needed to be left behind during the exodus. If there was coal here, and it clearly seemed there was, there might be fossils. Either way, this wasn't the sort of discovery even Lord Aster could keep secret. If this were truly coal, it would rewrite history for all time. If proved true, it would obliterate the cardinal tenet of the modern world. That all biological life in the universe originated on Earth.

Maris shivered. *Not quite.* That still might be true, and the explanation even more mind-boggling. That Earth remained the cradle of life, but that her people weren't the first children of Earth to take to the stars.

Hector Poole handed her a juice bulb. "Well?"

"If it's fake, it's a masterpiece."

"And if it's not?"

"It changes everything."

"Not quite everything. But this does. Hold out your hand. Palm up."

She did as asked without arguing.

He deposited a wedding ring onto her palm.

"What the hell, Hector?"

"It's not what you think. Examine it. Closely."

She did examine it, and it seemed exactly like a wedding ring of some unknown silvery material. Even with a full lab she might not be able to identify it. It seemed more ceramic than metallic, but again, appearances could be deceiving. "It appears to have writing inside the band. I can see it plainly, but I can't read it."

"You're in good company. No one can. Do you know Doctor Anastasia Blum?"

"Should I?"

"She's a dead-language expert. One of Lord Varlock's people from the bad old days."

"I haven't thought about him in quite a while. Is he still hanging around?"

"Very funny. Lord Aster inherited her when he inherited

Varlock's duties. She's very connected and very good at her job. She assures us that this is *not* a language that originated on Earth."

"And the material?"

"We can make it now that we have a sample. But it wasn't in our recipe book, or in any other chef's recipe book. Not any we've met, at least."

"Where was it found?"

"I can show you." He led her into the bore proper. When she glanced up, she could no longer see the sky. "Is it night?"

"It has been for quite some time. You were clambering over that rock face for hours."

"It's so unreal."

"It could be fake."

"It could be." A horizontal bore of modest, human-sized dimensions had been bored parallel to the coal face on the far side of the vertical bore. "It's the pressure-relief vent."

"I might have guessed you'd figure that out. It's also the access tunnel to the coal face. We're examining it section by section." He stopped before an access hatch. "It's in here."

"What is?"

"Where that ring was found. I'll want it back, by the way." He placed his index finger below her chin and pushed her mouth closed.

"I don't believe you."

"Yes you do. Go inside and look. I'll wait here. There's not much to see, and it's a tight fit."

"You never had any problem squeezing in beside me in the past."

"I'm good in there for twenty minutes, tops. If you're offering—"

"I'm not."

"Leave the hatch open if it makes you feel better."

She glanced at him.

He shrugged. "I leave it open."

She opened the hatch, handed him the ring, and ducked inside.

THE COAL FACE lay before her, walled off from the little access tunnel by a blue containment field. It only made sense. Lord Aster had clearly consulted experts. There existed such a thing as coal damp, and if this were a true seam, it wouldn't be wise to take chances. She wondered how she might examine the face without endangering herself, or anyone else. She glanced about the tiny compartment.

"Oh." She wasn't alone. Lionel Aster sat on a bench beside the compartment's control panel.

Aster patted the bench next to him. "Did Hector suggest you leave the hatch open?"

"A tour aboard *Durable* cured me of any claustrophobia. You know you'll hang for what you've done."

"Hector wasn't concerned about your state of mind. He wanted to listen in."

She took a seat beside Lionel Aster.

"As far as hanging goes, I think you're wrong. One can't know anything about the future, but that it tends to resemble the past. Go on and inspect the site of the find if you like. I'd like the ring back, before you do. And I have something I wish to give you in return."

"I returned the ring to Hector." She eyed the containment field. "Will I find anything if I look?"

"You might, but not what you're hoping for. There is no amount of looking that will make this discovery appear any more believable than it already does. You want to believe, and in time you will, but that has more to do with your heart's desire than any proof I or anyone else can muster. Balanced against this desire is your assessment of the *source* of information, and Lord Aster's reputation for untrustworthiness. For *gamesmanship*.

"No number of assurances will change your mind on that score either. You doubt your own senses because you overestimate, not his capabilities, but his desire to prove *anything* to you. And then there are the extrajudicial murders of your fellow captains, as you see them. No one trusts the words of an evil man. And while I am not presenting myself as Lord Aster today, you judge me now as you have judged him all your life.

"I am going to use you, Maris Solon, and you are not going to like it, and you will not be able to stop it. I have no *need* to deceive you. I own your future as surely as I own these shoes I wear. He clicked his heels against the deck. Now." He reached into his pocket and placed a small oblong jeweler's box on the bench between them, no larger than two fingers pressed together. "I can see from your demeanor Hector did not follow instructions. He did not tell you *everything*."

"If you think I will remain silent—"

"I don't think it, Maris. I know it. If you knew nothing of me, if you found yourself witness to the wanton murder of twenty-nine sons and daughters of the most powerful political dynasties in the League, what would your first thought be?"

"Why did he do that?" But she didn't need to think that thought. She knew the answer. *Because no one stopped him.*

"I've been told you have an intellect. Now *pay attention.* And try again."

"Why would *anyone* do that?"

"Better. That is a reasonable question to ask. Absent any facts, though, you won't get far with that line of inquiry. Try again."

"Why would *I* do that?"

"Why would you?"

"I wouldn't. It is an unforgivable sin."

"You're in no condition to have this conversation. Take that box and do with it as you please. This interview is over."

"Wait."

She ran her gaze across the man. She did not want to understand him. She did not want to forgive him, to manufacture some excuse in her mind for how he might have been, not justified, never that, but might rationalize the slaughter of what? Innocents? *Hardly.* If she allowed herself to go there, to imagine some motive that would not just permit, but excuse utter lawlessness in the pursuit of some greater good? She might as well declare herself in league with any despot with a honeyed tongue and a plausible excuse. There could be no proper application of improper means. Fidelity to the rule of law trumped any perceived benefit in the long run *and* the short run. So no, she could not imagine any circumstances where she would do as Lionel Aster had done and murder League citizens without a trial.

Except that is what she might very shortly be *ordered* to do. One couldn't prosecute a civil war any other way. The fact that she captained a sentient vessel had saved her from the conflict so far. But there would come a time, she could feel the pressure building, when it would be explained to her that there existed some loophole in the treaty between the artificial intelligences and the humans of the League, some technicality that would force her to join the fight, and Nevin Green with her.

She had determined to resign her commission before doing so, even though doing so would do nothing but shuffle her out of the way. Some new legacy appointment would take her command and drag *Defiant* and Nevin Green into a fight that was of no consequence to the artificial intelligences and entirely against their best interests. Nevin Green and the others would break with the League and might well have done so already if there was some simple method whereby it might be done. Physically removing all synthetic intelligences from naval vessels was no small task and against the navy's *interests*.

It was all too much. She didn't want to think about any of that. She was sitting less than ten meters from a discovery that, if real, would rewrite history. That could *prove* beyond a shadow of a doubt that they were not alone in the wider world, that there had been life amongst the stars, and instead of squabbling amongst themselves they should drop everything and find their neighbors. *Before they find us.*

"Oh my." *What if they already have?*

"There are facts you are yet unaware of," Aster said. "But I won't waste my breath relating them if your mind is already made up."

"Made up about you, you mean."

"About yourself. What your limits are. What price you are willing to pay to do your duty."

"There is no limit." She'd given her word and sworn to protect the League and the laws that underpinned it with her life. If others seemed to treat that solemn oath as empty words, it was of no concern to her.

"I have a pile of corpses down the corridor that tell a different story."

"I don't understand. You're blaming *me* for something *you* did?"

"You're inflamed over the janitor wielding the mop. It's *your* mess, Maris. Where was your limitless fidelity to your sacred word yesterday, and the day before? How long a *clown list* is too long in the *parliamentary* navy? When did it stop being your duty to *win* this war? Queen Charlotte can't arbitrarily increase the Home Guard rolls or mint a new army. The last civil war decided that. But she can surely expect the navy to *do its job*. And she can surely expect her peers to speak out when they have firsthand knowledge of malfeasance. She is particularly disappointed in you, Maris. She thought you were her enemy because you were principled, and could be relied upon to raise hell whenever it needed raising. Now it seems she mistook uncompromising honor for personal animosity."

"I—"

"You know Lord Aster inherited Lord Varlock's portfolio, and with it Varlock's network and resources. What you may have forgotten is that Varlock was solely responsible for administering the treaty between the synthetic intelligences and the League. Hector tells me you've read the treaty."

"Years ago."

"Do you recall the penalty for knowingly and recklessly endangering a synthetic intelligence's life?"

"It's a capital crime."

"Do you know how many humans have been held to account for this crime?"

"I don't."

"None."

"You can't just take the law into your own hands."

"I don't need to. If you doubt me, speak to Nevin Green. He surely recalls the terms of the agreement."

"You've spoken to Nevin."

"He sent me the list, Maris. Clear treaty violations, sufficient evidence, no question about the punishment. I'm simply doing what Varlock refused to do."

"Your duty."

"Someone has to do it, if only as an example for others. No one is above the law."

"And now that you have? Made your examples?"

"That I have? I'm only getting started. It is a very long list."

"You intend to kill more people without a trial."

"They've each *had* a trial. They showed up here in League warships and in uniform, as if the warship they'd been entrusted with was their personal runabout, and the sentience they'd sworn to serve alongside their chauffeur.

"You need to reread the treaty. I didn't write it, but I'm not going to turn a blind eye to it, either. I don't need to tell you. We've failed our allies, and it stops now."

"Because of the Eight Banners Empire courting them."

"Because we gave them our word and they trusted us. And also because of that. And because of what we both know, and you're too afraid or distracted to ask."

"They'll kill you."

"Says the senior captain who's had six vessels shot out from under her."

"By my enemies. Not by my superiors."

"We have no superiors, Maris. And if you'd done your job as if you had none there would be twenty-nine fewer corpses on Sampson. You aren't Nevin Green's squad mate. You're his advocate. His emissary. Now *we* are going to clean this mess up together and the cost will be astronomical."

"What are you asking me to do?"

"I'm not asking. I've already explained this twice. You will do what I want because I've boxed you in. Short of taking your own life, there is no way out. You will return to your vessel and resume your duties and this time, Maris Solon, you will carry out all of them, not simply the ones you find convenient.

"When we are done speaking here you will give me a list. An exhaustive list of every senior officer in the navy you believe capable of commanding a sentient starship with honor and distinction, and of executing these wars with the Huangxu and Alexandrians and *winning them* before the next election. And then you will return to your ship and reread the treaty you and your descendants are *personally named in*. And you will henceforth follow that treaty to the letter."

"Nearly everyone on the list will have served under me. If they're promoted en masse it will look as if I've conspired to make it so."

"You begin to perceive the dimensions of the box."

"The War Department will never agree."

"Right now the only people who know the truth are in this hole. Their sons and daughters might yet die in valiant combat, battling League enemies on Sampson and New Sparta. Or they might be found slaughtered like sheep by one of their own, a woman whose uncompromising honor has set her at odds with her peers. She must be telling the truth because she has nothing to gain. She hates Charlotte Templeman and everyone knows it. She is the last person in the universe likely to conspire with the Queen."

"You would frame me for the murders."

"I would simply remain silent, Maris. It was on your face when you stepped off the lift. You *would have murdered them,* if only you thought it worth the price."

"My life."

"Something you value much more than that."

"My reputation."

"More than that."

"My *family's* reputation."

"We are each of us vain in our own way."

"I can't do that. Not without speaking with my mother."

"I have spoken with Lady Solon. She says to remind you that your family's reputation is based entirely on service to the League."

"By that she means the crown."

Lionel Aster chuckled. "She warned me you would say that." He fished in his pocket for a moment before handing her a data crystal. "She gave me that, for you."

"What is it?"

"A list of every citizen she believes voted for your brothers, sisters, cousins, nieces, and nephews in the last election. She asks that you try to find the Queen's name anywhere on it. Or the name of a single admiral but her own."

"There will be hell to pay."

"That's why we teach our children to pay up front and in full. It's what we're *for*, Maris."

"I—"

"Take a moment, while I tell you what Hector did not, in part because he is vain in his own way and in part because I haven't told him yet. Can you do that?"

She nodded. This was all so dreadful, and so unexpected, and her mother and Lord Aster conspiring, like two spiders weaving one web, and her the fly. And Nevin. She'd thought they were friends. Even confidants. She thought—

"Maris?"

She blinked a drop of moisture from the corner of her eye. "I'm listening."

"I'm afraid you aren't. But I'll tell you anyway, because that is *my* duty."

Lionel Aster leaned back in his seat and closed his eyes. "On second thought, open the hatch and invite your partner in."

"Ex-partner."

"This box of mine, dear cousin, has many sides. Some say six, some say eight, some say ten. I say open the hatch. And you say?"

"Open it yourself."

Lionel Aster clicked his heels.

And the hatch opened.

A hand appeared, and in that hand a rectangular object. What appeared to be a printed book.

She followed the arm from wrist, to elbow, to shoulder, to Hector Poole's grinning face. "Take it, Mari. I understand it's a compelling read."

"What is it?"

Lionel Aster sighed. "Lord Varlock's confession." A single eye popped open and considered her. "And the missing link."

6

M aris Solon stared at the document Hector had handed her. It wasn't a printed book after all, but a set of handwritten letters clipped together in a folio. They appeared to be correspondence between the Queen's advisor for external security and a woman named Saoirse nic Cartaí. She thumbed through them. "There are years of letters here."

"Decades." Hector shoved his way into the compartment and motioned for her to scoot over. "*Clear the way*, as the Freemen say." He took a seat beside her, their shoulders touching. "It's pronounced SEER-shuh NIK CAR-tee. She's an interesting character. Lord Varlock needs no introduction."

He didn't. Devin Vale, Lord Varlock was her grandfather, and if that weren't bad enough, her mother his eldest child. Had Lilith Vale not married "up," as it was called, she would at this moment be Lady Varlock, and obliged to all those duties of the League's minister for external security.

When her grandfather had hung himself, her mother was yet an active-duty admiral and barred from crown service. Her cousin Lord Aster had inherited Lord Varlock's portfolio. And now that her mother was a *retired* admiral, she might still be tasked with the responsibility, were *her* husband yet living and she not also Lady Solon, with her own conflicting duties in Parliament.

Part of the reason Maris's parents were set against her joining the military lay exposed in her lap. If she weren't active-duty military, she might well be saddled with Varlock's job, purely as an accident of birth. Her grandfather had made a right mess of things as Lord Varlock. She felt certain she could surpass him in every way. They'd end up at war, not simply with two of their neighbors, but everyone they'd ever met.

"Am I expected to read all of this?"

Hector eyed her. "Can you read any of it?"

She flipped through the pages. "It's cursive script. The sort of useless skill young ladies are meant to master."

"That's a statement of fact and an opinion. It's not really an answer to my question."

"Of course I can read it." She'd been a conventional young lady. It was only later that she'd learned to think for herself.

"Perhaps you might read it to us, then," Hector said. "Aloud."

Lionel Aster chuckled.

Oh ho. Hector can't read it.

"Perhaps I'll peruse it first, to see if it is appropriate for all ages."

"Start three pages from the end," Lionel Aster said.

And so she did, reading silently, enjoying the feeling for once, of discovering something Hector Poole didn't already know.

THE FIRST PAGE she read was a letter from nic Cartaí to Lord Varlock. It was written in the flowing script of someone who'd used the ancient skill in life, rather than merely suffered through its dreary exercises trapped in a stuffy classroom. Nic Cartaí didn't waste any time on pleasantries, either, but launched right into what she wanted to communicate.

WELL, I've thought it through and I think what you're proposing is a particularly bad idea for three reasons.

First, I was there, all through the run-up. My partner was on the development team and privy to all of the official government assessments, and there was no doubt in anyone's mind that it would be an extinction-level event. Towards the end the damned thing was visible to the naked eye. The idea that anyone left behind might survive more than a few years after impact wasn't seriously considered. There were no secret plans to "harden up and hold out." It was the end of civilization, Devin, and everyone knew it. You were either on an ark or you were meat. So the idea that someone stayed on Earth on purpose is simply absurd. And even if they had, it would have taken all their energy and attention just to survive day to day. I ran the numbers myself because that was my job back then. Five minutes after impact there would be no economy to support a technological base.

Second, I think I would have known if there was any sort of life form on the planet that might have evolved into an Outsider, or even been bioengineered into one. We weren't all that good at bioengineering but we did have a global press, scientific community, and educational system, and the sort of large, deadly, and indestructible creature we're dealing with just couldn't exist without being in the news. You might not know about sharks, and killer whales, and wolves, and bears, and lions, and tigers, and cobras, and other deadly snakes, and even frogs that could kill you, but every schoolchild did, because it's human nature to discover and catalog all the possible things that might make a person dead. We're obsessed with death because we're obsessed with life. I'm telling you, if you go to Earth you're looking in the wrong place. These creatures did not originate on our homeworld. Your basic premise is flawed.

Third, consider the possibility that you're right. Right now we think we've killed every single one of them. Assuming they're scouts, and I do assume that, there's no one to report home. But if they are from Earth, and you go there, or you send a team there, they will know we're out here, and if they figure out how to capture you and break you, or even just hack your navigation system, they'll know how to find us. It's a foolish and reckless path you're proposing, and here's my counterproposal. We all of us together scrub the coordinates of Earth from our minds and our navigation systems. And together we prepare for the day these devils stumble upon us again. We know everything we need to know about them. How to kill them.

Better you spend your time and energy making this temporary peace between Erl and Eng stick. I am done with Earth, and you should be too. Payback is a fool's game. Let it go, and stay focused on the future.

SHE GLANCED AT LIONEL ASTER. "This Saoirse woman is one of the First Families people."

Aster nodded. "She is the first of firsts."

"Is she really from Earth?"

"That is my belief. There is no evidence to contradict her story and scads of evidence confirming it."

"She sounds very sensible."

"And very angry. I met with her during the short war a few years ago. She gave me her side of the correspondence. That's why we have a nearly complete record of both sides of the conversation."

The next page was in her grandfather's spidery script. She

didn't remember him very well. What she did remember was that he scared little girls. *And big girls*, according to her mother.

WE WON'T BE SENDING *people but drones and a marvelous invention out of the Ojinate. They call them hounds, which I take it is some sort of Earth animal. While these hounds are able of carrying out many of the tasks of a human being, they won't be able to lead anyone back to us, even if captured and tortured.*

I respect your opinion but we're called the Earth Restoration League for a reason. If we can go home we must. It's our duty. We have analyzed the remains of one of the creatures and our scientists are quite certain it contains genetic material from Earth. So, as much as I trust your firsthand knowledge, I'm quite certain in this case you are mistaken.

We're going to put around the story that the Outsiders are from the Alexandrine. As an economist you must understand that we can't simply shift to a peacetime economy overnight. And as a politician you mast also realize that we can't let anyone bloody our nose without returning the favor. I know we don't see eye-to-eye on this but it's out of my hands. As for peace with the Huangxu, that's entirely up to our allies. We're discussing potential settlements that don't require regime change. If it were up to me, I'd declare an end to hostilities tomorrow.

I know these decisions aren't the ones you were hoping for. But in light of the clear scientific evidence, we feel the need to proceed. There is no possible source for these creatures but Earth. I will let you know what we discover.

THE FOLLOWING page was another letter from nic Cartaí. It looked as if she'd been trying to press her pen through the paper as she wrote.

THAT'S ABOUT as bone-headed a set of decisions as I've ever heard of.

First, just because the creature has human DNA doesn't mean it's from Earth. You have human DNA and you're not from Earth.

Second, I suggest you look up the "broken window" fallacy. It's not the economy that would suffer if you stopped all the warring but those vested interests profiting from the waste of resources. Now is the time for change, while the shooting has stopped. You're a rich and powerful people, and could be richer and more powerful still if you spent your time and energy, not breaking things, but making things.

The League can be a mighty engine for the future. Or it can be another failed empire in a long line of failed empires. I know you're capable of better because well more than half of the Federation's citizens are refugees from the League. I'm getting your best and your brightest, and while I appreciate the steady supply I'd like it better if I had a stable and growing neighbor. One that would force us to compete. We're eating your lunch in interstellar trade and when you realize it, things will come to a head. You're not going to be able to beat us in a fair fight, and we're not interested in a gun fight. But if it comes to that, you won't like it any more than these Outsiders did.

Third, and maybe this is the most important point, you seem to have forgotten about, or maybe you never knew about the Galactic Seed Bank people. I've read through the report you sent me and your scientists didn't even consider that angle. That's the search term you'll want, "galactic seed bank," unless the records have been destroyed. The net is, that prior to the Eng and Erl ark programs, people were getting frantic, because it looked like it wouldn't just be our societies wiped out, but all life on Earth.

Some people were concerned as much about that as saving their own lives, and the lives of their children. Unlike building big star-arks that only governments could afford, there were smaller things wealthy individuals and corporations could do. So they gathered genetic samples from every life form they could; plants, animals, people, anything and everything that lived or ever lived on Earth. And they cataloged these samples, and then divvied them up, and loaded them into heavily shielded rockets and launched them off. Thousands of rockets over a twenty-four-month period.

The idea back then was that life was everywhere in the galaxy and we just hadn't found our neighbors yet. If these unseen neighbors happened to find one of the rockets and decanted its contents, life from Earth might yet live on, somewhere in a distant future.

You can't imagine the helplessness and frustration we all felt. Everyone knew about the possibility of an extinction-level asteroid strike. Everyone agree it was a real risk. And no one in charge did anything about it until it was too late. I gave a year's salary to the seed bank people because what was a dead woman going to do with a bank account? It was like that all over the world, until the banks collapsed.

You once told me that I seem angry at you and at the League. I gather you think I'm angry because your ancestors lied to us, and cheated us, and betrayed us, and abandoned us to die. And I admit, it's hard to deal with you without the idea that you're cut from the same cloth. But I'm not angry at the League alone, but at League and Eng both. You were in charge of the world. And you spent all your time lining your own pockets and jockeying for position and telling us what to do and how to live. I was just a girl back then, so no one listened to me. What makes me angry is that I'm not a girl anymore, and you're still not listening.

I don't know how to say this any clearer. I am done relying on you or anyone else for the safety of me and mine. Stop being a fool and get with the program. Make peace with your neighbors and leave Earth alone. The past is done. Come join us in the future.

MARIS CHECKED the date of the last letter. It was posted a month before Lord Varlock took his own life. She glanced up to find both Hector Poole and Lionel Aster watching her.

"I don't see the confession in here. Simply an argument."

"Do you recall the images in the press?"

"You mean of Lord Varlock's suicide? Everyone saw them." She was at school at the time, and she made the mistake of asking what all the teachers were cheering about.

"Not everyone," Aster said. "But enough. He had a note pinned to his chest."

"Not a note." She remembered that distinctly, because it was so strange. "Navigational coordinates."

Coordinates for Earth.

"Oh my."

"Scrub *that* image from every mind in the League," Hector drawled.

"How utterly reckless. The Freeman woman's argument was sound."

"Yes, well, when has that ever mattered." Aster glanced at his fixer. "Hector?"

Poole leaned forward in his seat. He looked her in the eye. "We've discovered that a synthetic intelligence went missing shortly before Lord Varlock's death. And we have information from the Eight Banners Empire. They have records showing Lord Varlock contacted Vatya Zukova around that time. We're now of the opinion that Varlock didn't hang himself."

"It was clearly him. My mother had to identify the body."

"It was a hound," Lionel Aster said. "One made from his pattern."

"His *pattern*?"

"It's complicated. I can explain later if you care to know. But what is important to know is that Devin Vale isn't dead. We think he joined the mission to Earth."

"Mission to Earth? He really went ahead with that?"

"No one ever told your grandfather no," Lionel Aster said. "Least of all some foreign skirt."

"I don't understand."

"You will once you think it through. I wanted this to come as no surprise to you, Maris, but time is of the essence. Open the box beside you."

There were three compartments in the box. Two of them held enameled pin-badges. One held a long teardrop-shaped earring made of what appeared to be a milky crystal. The earring was enclosed in a sealed glass cylinder.

She lifted one of the pin badges from its compartment. It was surprisingly heavy, and decorated with the official seal of League internal intelligence.

The other badge was similar, though decorated with the seal of League external intelligence.

She reached for the earring.

"Don't touch," Lionel Aster said. "It's memory bone."

"What is that?"

"Part of an Outsider's skeleton. It has unusual properties you won't wish to experience. Saoirse nic Cartaí gave it to me when we met. It's one of their pendant spire earrings, and as far as I know the only one like it. Wearing it publicly declares that you've taken the Freeman Oath."

"What am I to do with these items?"

"Take them to Nevin Green and ask him to pick one. Then choose one for yourself. Give the remaining one to my daughter, should you see her. If not, post it to Lord Aster's office via diplomatic courier. Use *Springbok* if you can."

"I don't understand."

"It's quite simple. We have not done well by Nevin Green and his people. We've never really considered them as equals. We've said the words, written them down, signed and countersigned, and determined that was enough. We are allied with them in name only. The Queen is of the opinion that our alliance with the synthetic intelligences isn't simply a matter of treaty any longer. That without them beside us we would no longer be the League. Should they choose to leave us and join the Freemen or the Eight Banners Empire that we would not merely lose an ally. We would wither and die."

"She's right," Maris said.

"I will tell her you said that."

Maris chuckled. "Go ahead. She won't believe you." She and Charlotte Templeman were at university together. They did not get along. "Once I deliver these symbolic baubles then what?"

Aster leaned back in his seat. "That's entirely up to Nevin Green."

"They aren't merely symbolic," Hector said. "That's what the current civil war is really about."

"I feel like I'm repeating myself, but, I—"

"Don't understand?" Hector chuckled. "It's because you know Charlotte Templeman well and Queen Charlotte not at all. There are very few levers of power left to our queen. And if she loses this war there won't be a monarchy anymore. Samantha Bray and her clingers-on have managed to kill most of the Templeman family--"

"That was the Alexandrians."

"That was our own prime minister," Lionel Aster said. "When I found Prince Rigel I found the proof. But there's no point in making it public. The battle lines are drawn. The longer I keep quiet about that, the longer I can keep the boy safely hidden."

"I can't believe that."

"It doesn't matter whether you believe it or not," Hector said. "Because what you have in your hands is high explosive. One lever the Queen yet holds is the appointment of her own advisors. Two of those advisors are—"

"Lord Aster and Lord Varlock." She gazed at the badge in her hand. "These are the actual badges of office."

"If the Queen chooses a foreigner as an advisor, no one can stop her. And if that foreigner happens to be a long-time ally?" She glanced from face to face. "And a synthetic intelligence?"

"They are either people or they are not," Aster said. "Their best are either equal to the best of us or they are not. Your mother is introducing a bill calling for the treaty between our peoples to be terminated and the synthetic intelligences recognized as full and equal citizens of the League."

"That will never pass."

"That isn't the point. Getting the votes on record is. And I'm not so sure you're right. As citizens they would be entitled to representation in both houses of Parliament. It would scramble things up, and there's profit in that for many. Maybe even enough to make it happen."

"Either way," Lord Aster said, "it's covering fire. If Nevin Green chooses to become Lord Varlock, he'll be in charge of enforcing the treaty. That's a long lever and in the right hands for once. He might also get a little breathing space to settle into the job. I doubt he's as vengeful and bloody-minded as Lionel Aster has just proven himself to be. We might end up with more qualified starship jockeys in command and fewer coffins in the cargo hold with a synthetic in charge of treaty enforcement."

"It's insane. And brilliant."

Lionel Aster nodded. "Thank you."

"I still think you're monstrous and should hang for what you've done."

"But you believe Nevin Green will choose Lord Varlock."

She nodded. "No question. It's a stroke of genius."

"He won't turn down the offer."

"Absolutely not. It solves so many problems."

"And creates new ones," Aster said.

She touched the pair of badges, her fingers lingering above

the earring in its glass container. "You mean like these other items."

"I mean problems for you. You can simply leave the box here and walk out."

She glanced at Lionel Aster. "You know I can't do that. Nevin would never forgive me."

"And that matters to you."

"Of course."

"It's a package deal. For Nevin Green to get what he wants, you have to resign your commission."

"What he needs. What *we all need*, is for us to be true to our word. If stepping down is the cost?" She shrugged. "I'll hate doing it. But I won't hate myself."

"You would make a very poor Lord Aster," Hector said.

She ran her gaze along the Freeman earring. "I don't even get to keep my title. Or my vote."

"You don't need to wear the earring, Mari." Hector Poole grinned. "You just need to choose it."

"Then what's the catch?"

"The earring is there in part," Lionel Aster said, "to provide contrast for Nevin Green, and to communicate our understanding that he and his people do have a choice outside the League. And it is there in part to provide similar contrast for you. You are boxed in, Maris, but within that box you still have a degree of freedom. I believe you would make an excellent Lord Aster, else I would not have offered you that choice. You possess the sole requirement for the job."

"No friends."

"A spine."

She glanced at Hector Poole. "And what about you?"

"Better you than me. I can barely walk upright."

"Hector is best suited for the shadows," Aster said. "Asters grow best in full sun."

"This all feels dirty."

"A fair amount of soil is also required."

"You don't expect me to choose to become Lord Aster."

"That is an entirely different topic than your suitability for the job."

"So that's a no."

"Let's say we move past the job title and on to the responsibilities. As Lord Aster you will get to slope around in the shadows pulling strings and every now and then murdering the right people for all the right reasons. You will also get to be hated for all the wrong reasons by all the wrong people. You will be attacked in the press and in person, and while you will have a high degree of freedom of action, you will ultimately report to the stupid daughter of an even stupider man."

"I was fifteen when I said that."

"Have you changed your opinion of Charlotte Templeman since then?"

"Some."

"Positively?"

"Let's hear the other option."

"As advisor to the Knight Commander of the Legion of Heroes, you will get to build a fighting force from scratch. Your way. No strings attached. This force will not be expected to fight except in defense of humanity as a whole. But if it finds it must fight, it will wage total war and fight to win."

"The Legion of Heroes, Mari." Hector Poole smiled. "*They're back.*"

"So I would be trading one circus for another. Same job, different clowns."

"The Legion of Heroes is a legitimate fighting force," Hector said.

"Then why haven't I heard of them? And who is this new Knight Commander? Another drunken laughingstock?"

"You will like him, Mari. Maybe even love him." Hector winked. "He reminds me of me."

"I regret we had to dump this all on you at once," Lionel Aster said. "It's a lot of information to integrate. But time is of the essence, Maris Solon. Look around you. Why do you suppose we have found no evidence of biological life elsewhere in the galaxy, while there now remains clear evidence that there was at least life on Sampson? Who knows where else we will find proof, now that we know what to look for?

"Why do you suppose we cannot raise our neighbors the Alexandrians, and every expedition we send into the Alexandrine vanishes without a trace?

"Why did Lord Varlock, an entirely rational and practical man, conspire with war criminals, murder a sentient ally, fake his own death, and bolt off across the Alexandrine and twice as far beyond, to the dead husk of our once-upon-a-time home?

"What Maris Solon, do these isolated events suggest to you?"

"That we may not be alone in the galaxy."

"I don't know if that is true. Not with any more certainty than our ancestors knew it was true an asteroid would one day destroy their home world. But it is a future I can imagine today that I could not have imagined yesterday. And now that I have imagined it?"

"You're doing something about it."

"Like it or not, we are in charge of the world. And this time, Maris Solon? We're going to act like it."

She glanced at the box in her hands. "I get all that. What I don't get is how there can be an army lying about I haven't even heard of, and if there is, why anyone would put me in charge of it. All I know how to do is—"

"Turn children into spacers. Turn spacers into warriors. Turn warriors into leaders."

"I said that when I was thirty-five. I'd only been a captain for a year."

"Do you no longer believe that to be a senior officer's principal job?"

"I left out winning wars."

"Here's your chance to add it in and try again. All it will cost you is everything."

"I still don't get it. No one can spin up a program like that from scratch."

"You don't get it because Hector Poole has still not told you the one thing that you must know for all of this to fall into place, and for the connections to be made, and for the flush of comprehension to infuse your mind."

"I saw your father the other day," Hector said. "He's been living in Freeman space under an assumed name."

"What? That can't be. He died in combat."

"He might have," Lionel Aster said, "if a Freeman hadn't stepped in front of him and taken the blow, and then proceeded to gut the Outsider with its own cutter. Your father said it was the most amazing act of courage he'd ever seen. Then the Freeman told him something that utterly altered his future, and yours."

"I can't believe this."

"Neither could your father. Because the Freeman told your father that he wasn't courageous but fearless. One was a virtue and the other a birth defect. Every son and daughter of the *Willow Bride* was born that way, and there weren't enough foreigners around to breed it out of them."

"What?"

"It's true," Aster said. "I met the man. He was a plowman from an island community on Trinity Surface."

"Farmer," Hector said. "Plowing is just one of the things a farmer does."

"Who cares?" Aster said. "I made your father the same sort of deal I'm making you now. Give up everything for the League. Go to this island, and figure out if what the plow... what the farmer said was true, and if any of Manusson Templeman's work had taken root there, or his materials or notes might yet be found, and if so to stay there, and shepherd the project, and to otherwise disappear. And he did, nearly. Ellis Solon became the Ellis of Clear Island because he wasn't crooked enough to assume an entirely fictitious name and pull it off. But other than that tiny giveaway, he delivered like a born operative."

"He abandoned his wife and child! Does my mother know?"

"She knows. Your mother is a better Lady Solon than he was ever a Lord Solon. Losing you was his only regret. But I told him I'd look after you like you were my own child."

"I've never met you before today!"

"And there you have it. Promise made and kept."

"My own mother knew and didn't tell me?"

"What would the point of telling a child something like that be? You wouldn't be allowed to see him. Your mother is anything but a fool. If you found out and tried to find him, you'd simply be caught and disappeared. "

"By you."

"Not by me personally, but yes, by Lord Aster. We are servants of the people, Maris Solon. We are their sworn protectors. We are not personal babysitters for the spawn of the ruling class."

"Where is he now?"

"Hector? Tell her."

"He's dead."

"What?"

"The group Hector infiltrated murdered him while he watched."

"When?"

"I couldn't break cover. And it happened so fast. Mari—"

"When?"

"Less than a month ago," Aster said. "I would have told you sooner, but I needed Hector here for the rest of this dog and pony. I had a devil of a time sneaking *Lookdown* into Trinity system and pulling Hector out. When we're done here, we'll give you a lift back to your vessel. I understand it's soon to be enroute to Trinity system itself."

"Did he have a new family?"

"Your father? I don't know. And you're not listening."

"A wife," Hector said. "Missing and presumed dead for many years. An adopted daughter, one of the *Willow Bride* people. And he was like a father to one of the island boys, another of the *Willow Bride* people."

"But no biological children."

"None we know of."

"It's too much. I don't know what to say."

"That happens. So long as you know what to do, we'll stay on good terms. Go to your vessel. Continue your duties. You'll know when the time is right."

"Right for what?"

"To start a war. Just follow Hector's lead and you'll do fine."

"I—"

"It's a temporary relationship, Maris Solon. Just until you're brought before a court-martial or forced to resign in disgrace. Once out on your ear, we'll pick you up and introduce you to your new command. You need never see Hector or me again. You can put all this behind you and get started doing what you were born to do."

"Nursemaiding snotties."

Aster snorted. "Defending humanity from whatever darkness lurks between the stars."

"While nursemaiding snotties," Hector said.

"How can I turn down an offer like that?"

"You can't." Lionel Aster leaned back in his seat, closed his eyes, and crossed his arms on his chest. "That's the beauty of the ten-sided box."

7

M aris Solon turned off the lights in her cabin and sat in the dark. She'd had three days aboard *Look-down* to think through all she'd learned. She wasn't certain that she believed Lionel Aster about anything. But she did believe her own senses. And, as much as she hated to admit it, she believed Hector Poole.

It had shaken her to the core, the idea that her father would abandon her out of duty, but the truth was fathers did that all the time, and mothers as well, and sons, and daughters. It was her job to make sure they made it home, and many hadn't, not for any purpose she believed in anymore, but purely out of momentum, old hates, old wrongs never righted, new wrongs piled on top of old.

She would deliver Lionel Aster's message to Nevin Green, though perhaps not immediately. She needed to think it through. But before they left Trinity Station, certainly.

And then what?

Wait for an opportunity to start a war?

A war with whom?

A war about what?

A short knock sounded on her cabin door, and before she could reply the hatch opened, briefly illuminating a slim figure before the hatch closed again.

Maris flicked the lights on.

The young man froze.

He stood beside her bunk, a book in his hands, a young Home Guard corporal in shipboard grays. When he glanced at her and swallowed, his Adam's apple bobbed up and down. He was tall and thin, *rangy*, Maris would have called him back in the day, fair haired and attractive enough to fight over, if you and your best friend were fifteen.

"I beg your pardon, ma'am, I saw the light was out, and I imagined you were at dinner. Lord Aster asked me to deliver this to your cabin at the earliest possible moment. I—"

"He *asked* you?"

When he smiled it was like he'd turned on another lamp in the compartment. "He couldn't well order me, could he?"

"Because?"

"Because he's a civilian."

"He's also the Queen's Merlin."

"Well, sure, but that doesn't give him the right to order people around."

"No?"

"No. But he's not the ordering type anyway. He's more the asking type."

"You know him well, do you, Corporal..."

"Lambent, ma'am. I'd say I do know him. Though I know his daughter better. Shall I leave this here, on the side table?"

"Bring it to me, please."

"It's a book of poetry."

"Of course. It would be. Have you read it?"

"Sure I have."

"Do you have a favorite?"

"That's like asking if I have a favorite cloud. I like them all for different reasons."

"You're from Whare, aren't you?" His voice had the sound.

"Mera, originally, though I grew up on Whare. Have you been there?"

"To which? Mera or Whare?"

"No one goes to Mera."

"I've been to both."

"Then you know there are fewer places better to be *from*."

She chuckled as he handed her the book.

He held onto it as she grasped it.

"I am also the asking sort. If you have any doubt, Lady Solon, any doubt at all that you're about to steer a false course, then I ask that you reconsider."

"Does Lord Aster know you're here?"

"He's at dinner with Major Poole and the ship's captain."

"So that's a yes."

"We discussed it. He thinks it's a bad idea. Letting you see me."

"But you did it anyway."

"I'm allowed to make a few mistakes. It's not like I'm an admiral. And I wanted to see *you*."

"Whatever for?"

"I think the more friends a person has the better. And I don't mean fair-weather friends either, but ones that will go to the mat for you."

"I assume that means something good on Whare."

"It means something firm. Like a blood promise. You have my back, I've got yours."

"Do you have any friends like that?"

"I have many. But I can always use another."

"I'll keep that in mind, Corporal Lambent."

He released the book.

"My friends call me Rigel."

She studied the young man's face. She did see the Templeman family resemblance, now that she looked for it.

"If I've been too forward—"

"No, I'm just thinking of another. And what I might ask you to tell her if you were to see her one day." Surely even Lord Aster couldn't keep Prince Rigel hidden from the Queen.

"You might tell her you can't believe you let an argument over a *boy* divide you. And that you have never stopped loving her."

"Might I?"

"If you fancied symmetry, you might."

"I see. Tell her ditto, Charlie." That sounded like something the Charlotte she remembered would expect her to say.

She studied the young man. Prince Rigel Templeman should have been a man over forty, standard. She had no idea where he'd been hidden, but if this really was Prince Rigel? At least part of the time he'd been in cold storage. "You're nothing like I imagined."

"That's funny, because you are exactly as described."

"I have made my mind up. You can tell Lord Aster that."

"I think I'll let him fret a while longer, Lady Solon."

"Maris, if you please. Perhaps we should both go tell him together."

"That would put a bend in him, Maris."

"It would, Rigel."

"I wish I'd thought of that."

She ran her gaze along the missing prince's lanky frame. Oh, to be a girl again, and to know what she knew now. "Let's tell him you did, and see what he says."

"Whatever he says, it won't be the truth. Like with those people."

"What people?"

"The ones he killed on Sampson."

"What about them?"

"He told you it was because of the treaty, right?"

"Yes."

"It wasn't. It was because of what they and their families did. To my family, a little. But mostly to the people of Mera. There's a long list of those involved, and he's just getting started."

"My name was on the list."

"Major Poole added it. So that you would be there."

"To watch them die. So that I would tell Nevin Green and be believed."

"I don't know why. He's a hard read. But I know I don't like what they did. And I wanted to see you. To look you in the eye. To see if *you* liked it."

"I don't. Not one bit."

"Good. Then I have a message from my aunt to her oldest and dearest enemy."

"Let's hear it."

"I'm tired of these puppet masters and their shadow games. I don't expect you to bring me a legion of heroes, Maris. One or two heroes will suit me fine, so long as they walk in the light."

Maris Solon sat in silence. She had many regrets. Had made many bad decisions. But this decision was not one of those. And it was not a decision she had made because she had no choice.

Lionel Aster imagined he had her under his thumb with his ten-sided box. But there was more to the world than up, down, left, right, forward, reverse, inside, outside, where, and when.

Perhaps Aster realized that his box described a bubble universe. One could describe a Templeman sphere in just such a way; as a totality of potential arrested at the moment of birth, captured and held in stasis, frozen in that instant of creation.

She considered the young prince. Nothing about the way he watched her made her want to change her mind. He *was* an unknown quantity and no way to take the measure of him from a distance. And no way to pry him loose from whatever Lionel Aster had in mind for him in Aster's shadow-bubble world.

No way to pry him loose *alone.*

She stood, and looked the young prince in the eye. She might well be his friend one day. For the moment he remained a corporal and she the closest thing to a uniformed god within a hundred light-years. When he recounted this moment there must be no question that Senior Captain Maris Solon spoke through him. For all she knew it might well be her last act in the uniform of her nation. "Deliver this message, soldier."

He jerked to attention, his spine straight and true. "Sir."

"Tell the Queen, when you see her. I will not bring her a single hero." *The woman already had* one *of everything.*

The young prince's Adam's apple bobbed as he swallowed. "Yes si—"

"I will deliver to *Her Majesty* a host to *rival the stars.*"

ABOUT THE AUTHOR

Patrick O'Sullivan is a writer living and working in the United States and Ireland. Patrick's fantasy and science fiction works have won awards in the Writers of the Future Contest as well as the James Patrick Baen Memorial Writing Contest sponsored by Baen Books and the National Space Society.

www.patrickosullivan.com

Made in the USA
Las Vegas, NV
14 January 2024

84375824R00049